THE HOUSE MOUSE

THE HOUSE MOUSE

BY DOROTHY JOAN HARRIS

Illustrated by Barbara Cooney

FREDERICK WARNE AND COMPANY, INC.

NEW YORK AND LONDON

In Canada: SAUNDERS OF TORONTO, LTD.

Copyright © Dorothy Joan Harris 1973
Illustrations Copyright © Barbara Cooney 1973
All Rights Reserved
Library of Congress Catalog Card Number: 72-89476
ISBN 0 7232 6096 6

Manufactured in the United States of America

1 2 3 4 5 6 7 8 9 10

To Kim and Douglas

The doll's house stood in the corner of Elizabeth's bedroom. Father had made it for her on her eighth birthday, but she didn't play with it. "Don't you like your doll's house?" Mother would ask. "Yes, I like it," Elizabeth would answer. But she never played with it. It sat there in the corner for months, and the only one to touch it was Mother, who dusted it on Fridays.

It was a beautiful doll's house. There was a downstairs and an upstairs, with a flight of real steps between, and the furniture was made of wood, painted red. The walls were all papered, there were white net curtains at every window, and little square rugs of velvet on the floor. The doll's bed had sheets and a tiny pillowcase, cut from an old hanky, and Mother had sewn a tiny quilt to go on top.

One Friday when Mother went to dust the doll's house, it looked different. The furniture had been moved about, and the little bed had been made up —not very neatly.

"Why, Elizabeth!" said Mother, "you've been playing with your doll's house."

"No," said Elizabeth, looking surprised.

"Well, someone was playing with it," said Mother.

"I was," said Jonathan, who was only four. "I was pretending my little rubber duck lived there."

"Ducks don't live in doll's houses," said Elizabeth.

"Mine does," said Jonathan.

"And boys don't play with doll's houses," said Elizabeth.

"I do," said Jonathan.

Father was surprised too, when he saw Jonathan playing with the doll's house. "Where's the little football I bought you?" he asked.

"In the toy box," answered Jonathan.

"Don't you want to go out and play with it?" asked Father.

"No, thank you," said Jonathan.

When Mother heard this, she just smiled and told Father, "He's only four—he's a bit young for football. Let him play what he wants."

So Father carried the doll's house into Jonathan's room and Jonathan played with it every day. At night he put his rubber duck to sleep in the bed; in the morning he made it go down the stairs—bump, bump, bump—and sit at the little red table for breakfast. Usually he would have a bit of cookie saved in his pocket to put on the table for its breakfast.

But it was then—when he started leaving bits of cookie on the little red table—that Jonathan noticed things happening in the doll's house. At first he just noticed that the bits of cookie kept disappearing from the little table. No matter how much cookie he left, it always disappeared.

Then he decided to watch the doll's house carefully. One night before he went to bed he looked at it for a long time. He tidied every room, and he left a whole cookie on the red table.

The next morning, as soon as he woke up, he jumped out of bed and ran to kneel in front of the doll's house. The cookie was gone. What's more, the bed was mussed and *one little red chair was knocked over!*

Jonathan looked at the chair for a long time. He looked at his rubber duck. Rubber ducks can't move. So who had knocked over the chair?

Jonathan didn't know, but he meant to find out.

That night he went to bed very early. Mother was surprised when she saw him already in his pajamas. "Are you sick?" she asked.

"No, I just want to go to bed now," said Jonathan.

"Are you that tired?"

"Yes," said Jonathan.

He wasn't tired really. But he wanted to get to sleep early so that he could wake up during the night and see what was going on in the doll's house. He often woke up during the night, even when he

11

didn't particularly want to—Mother had put a night-light in his room because of that. So now, when he had something special to wake up for, Jonathan was sure he could do it if he tried.

And he did. When he woke he lay still for a while, listening. Everyone was asleep. All the lights in the house were out except for his nightlight. Very quietly, Jonathan slipped out of bed. His feet made no sound on the carpet as he crept over to the doll's house. He knelt down and peeked in. There, curled up on the doll's bed, was a small brown mouse!

Jonathan sat very still, not making a sound. A mouse living in his doll's house! Would it run away when it saw him?

Very softly, he said, "Hello, mouse."

The mouse opened its eyes. But maybe because Jonathan was quite small himself, or maybe because he was very still and quiet—the mouse didn't seem afraid. It looked at Jonathan curiously.

"Hello," whispered Jonathan again.

"Hello," said the mouse in a small squeaky voice.

Perhaps if Jonathan had been older he would have been surprised to hear the mouse answer him. But as he wasn't any older than four, he wasn't surprised at all.

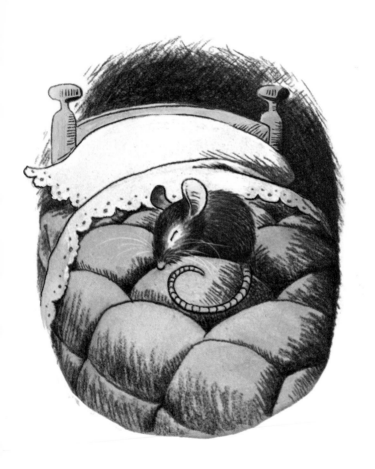

"Do you like my doll's house?" asked Jonathan.

"Doll's house?" said the mouse. "I don't see any dolls."

"Well, there aren't any in it," admitted Jonathan. "There's just my rubber duck—and you."

"Why can't it be my house then?" asked the mouse.

"I guess it can," said Jonathan.

"Good," said the mouse. It stretched its small furry legs and began to run up and down the little stairs.

"Do you come here every night?" asked Jonathan.

"Yes," said the mouse, "I like it here."

"Where do you stay during the day?"

"Oh, I have a hole in the attic with my family."

"*Our* attic?"

"Yes, my mother makes me stay up there during the day while there are people about." The mouse looked sharply at Jonathan. "Are *you* people?" it asked.

"I . . . I guess so," answered Jonathan.

"Then why are you awake now?"

"I wanted to see who was eating the cookies from the doll's house."

"Oh," said the mouse, "was it you who left the cookies?"

"Yes," said Jonathan.

15

"Well," said the mouse, "I liked the chocolate one best. I don't much care for plain ones. Do you think you can get some more fancy ones with cream filling?"

"I guess so," said Jonathan, rather surprised.

"Good," said the mouse. "Well, I'm tired. I think I'll go back to sleep now." And it curled itself up on the doll's bed again. Suddenly it opened one eye and looked up at Jonathan. "I forgot—thank you for the cookies," it said. Then it closed its eye again and was asleep in an instant.

Jonathan sat staring at the little brown furry ball curled up on his doll's bed. Then he shivered and climbed back into his own warm bed, and was soon asleep himself.

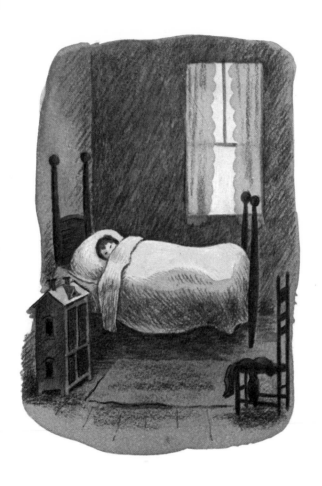

In the morning Jonathan looked at the doll's house for a long time. He could hardly believe that there had been a real mouse in it, talking to him, and sleeping on the doll's bed. But that night the mouse was there again. Jonathan had saved a chocolate chip cookie from lunch.

"Is this fancy enough?" Jonathan asked.

The mouse nibbled at a bit of chocolate. "Mmm, delicious!" it said, and ate up every crumb.

And so it went all winter. Every evening, Jonathan would go to bed very early, in order to visit with the mouse during the night. He brought it all kinds of fancy cookies—lemon creams, ginger snaps, ice cream wafers, and macaroons. The mouse gobbled them all up. Its table manners weren't very good and it didn't always remember to say 'thank you', but Jonathan didn't mind. He loved to watch the mouse's little soft whiskers quivering as it nibbled the crumbs.

"Where are all the cookies disappearing to?" Mother would ask. "The cookie jar is always empty."

"I'm not eating them," Jonathan would answer. And of course he wasn't.

"Yes, it was clever, wasn't it?" said the mouse, looking pleased with itself. "It's a very nice house," the mouse went on, looking around, "much nicer than the attic. It's warm, the bed has a soft quilt to sleep on, there are stairs to run up and down . . ."

"And there are cookies on the table," Jonathan added.

"Yes," admitted the mouse. "They make up for the scoldings. My mother scolds me every time I come home."

"You mean *mice* get scolded?" asked Jonathan, surprised.

"All the time," answered the mouse cheerfully. Then it looked at Jonathan sharply. "Why do you ask? *You* don't get scolded, do you?"

Jonathan nodded solemnly.

"Oh," said the mouse, with a very disappointed look on its little brown face. "Somehow I thought it would be different with people parents."

"And *I* thought it would be different with mouse parents," said Jonathan sadly.

Soon it was Christmas. Downstairs Father put up a big green tree, and they all trimmed it. At least, Mother and Elizabeth trimmed it.

"May I help?" Jonathan had asked.

"No," said Elizabeth.

"Yes," said Mother and handed him a shiny blue ball.

Jonathan reached up to put the ball on a high branch. Perhaps he reached too high, because, *crash!*

down fell the pretty blue ball. It broke into a hundred tiny pieces, all of them shiny blue.

"Oh Jonathan!" said Elizabeth, "I knew you'd break something."

"Never mind," said Mother, "it was an accident. How about putting on some tinsel, Jonathan?"

So Jonathan put tinsel on the low branches while Mother and Elizabeth trimmed the tree.

The next day, while Elizabeth was at school and Father was at work, Jonathan came to Mother. "Mummy," he said in a coaxing little voice, "could I have a small branch from the Christmas tree?"

"A branch? What for?" asked Mother.

"I want a little Christmas tree for the doll's house."

"All right," said Mother and got her scissors. She cut a small branch from the back of the tree where it wouldn't show and gave it to Jonathan.

"Thank you," said Jonathan and ran upstairs. He stuck the branch in a glob of plasticene to make it stand up and set it in the doll's house living room. Then he cut some tinsel into thin pieces and hung them on the tiny tree. It doesn't look much like a Christmas tree, thought Jonathan unhappily.

He went back downstairs. Some of the Christmas cards on the mantel were made of pretty shiny paper. "Mummy," he said again in his coaxing voice, "may I have a bit of shiny paper from one of the Christmas cards?"

Mother looked doubtful. "But Jonathan," she said, "we always leave the cards up until Christmas is over."

Jonathan looked up at Mother with sad eyes. "I just wanted a little piece to make some decorations for my Christmas tree," he explained.

"Well . . . all right," said Mother, handing him a shiny red card. "I guess one card less on the mantel won't matter."

Jonathan went back up to his room and cut out some balls and a star from the red paper. The star wasn't very good, but when they were all in place the tree looked quite pretty.

But it needs presents under it, thought Jonathan. And he went back downstairs again. "Mummy," he coaxed again, "may I have a little piece of Christmas ribbon? Just a little piece. And that's *all* I want."

Mother looked down at him and smiled. "Oh . . . all right," she said and snipped off a piece of gold ribbon for him.

Up Jonathan went again with the ribbon. He took the cookies he had saved from lunch out of his pocket—one strawberry cream and one big oatmeal wafer. Then he tied some ribbon around each cookie and put them under the little Christmas tree. Now the doll's house living room looked like his own. This time he sat back satisfied.

That night when Jonathan woke, the mouse was sitting looking at the tree. "What's that?" it asked.

"It's a Christmas tree," said Jonathan. "I made it for you."

"What's it for?" asked the mouse.

"Just to look pretty," said Jonathan, "and to put the presents under. Don't you think it's pretty?" he asked, disappointed.

"Oh yes, it's pretty," admitted the mouse. "And are these presents for me?" it asked, sniffing at the cookies.

"Yes," said Jonathan, "but you're supposed to save your presents until Christmas."

"Nonsense," said the mouse rudely, and began to nibble. It tried eating the ribbon too, but gave it up. "You can have the ribbon back now," it said to Jonathan.

It happened that the next night Mother read the children a bedtime story about a family of mice. These mice were all very polite and spent all their time either looking for cheese or running from the cat.

"That's a silly story," said Jonathan, when it was over. "Mice aren't polite. And they don't like cheese either."

"Don't they?" asked Mother. "What do they like?"

"Cookies," said Jonathan.

"How do you know?" asked Elizabeth.

"I just know," said Jonathan. But Mother looked at him rather strangely, as if she were wondering about something.

She looked at him the same way a few days later, when he took the little Christmas tree out of the doll's house.

"Are you throwing your tree out now?" she asked.

"Yes," said Jonathan, "Christmas is over."

"It was a pretty tree," said Mother.

"Yes," said Jonathan again, "but the mouse didn't like it."

"Mouse?" asked Mother quickly, "what mouse?"

"Oh . . . a pretend mouse who lives in the doll's house."

"A pretend mouse? Are you sure it's pretend?"

"Yes," answered Jonathan. "It's called Mr. Mc-Gillicuddy."

"Oh," said Mother, sounding reassured. "Well, if it's called Mr. McGillicuddy, I guess it's pretend, all right."

That night Jonathan told the mouse, "I've named you Mr. McGillicuddy."

"McGillicuddy?" squeaked the mouse angrily. "Nonsense! I never heard of such a ridiculous name!"

"Well, what name would you like?" asked Jonathan.

The mouse thought for a while. "I don't think I want a name," it announced at last. "I am Mouse, that's all."

"You're the House Mouse," said Jonathan.

"Exactly," said the mouse.

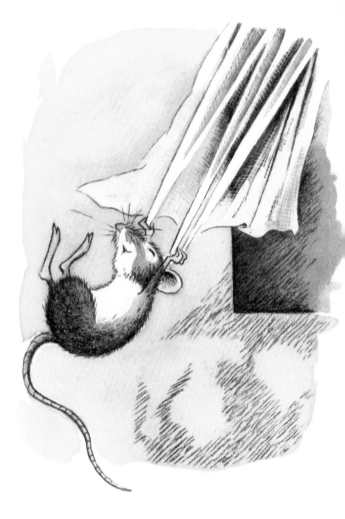

That winter went by quickly for Jonathan. He spent the days looking forward to his nightly visits with the mouse. Sometimes he even had a nap during the afternoon, if he was sleepy from getting up in the night. Mother was astonished when she found Jonathan lying down on his bed. "You haven't had an afternoon nap for years!" she said. "I'm tired," explained Jonathan, and went to sleep.

But the doll's house was beginning to look different. It didn't look so bright and clean any more. The mouse crumpled up the tiny quilt on the bed where it slept, and never tidied it up afterwards. It left cookie crumbs all through the house, and once it even tried swinging on the little white curtains. Jonathan tried to keep the house tidy. He smoothed out the quilt every day and cleaned up the cookie crumbs and tried to wipe off any paw marks from the floor. "You should wash your feet," he said the floor."

once to the mouse. "You're leaving footprints on

The mouse looked at Jonathan sharply. "If you're going to start scolding too . . ." it began.

"No," said Jonathan quickly. "I just thought a wash wouldn't hurt you, that's all."

"Humph," said the mouse rudely, and went right on mussing things up.

But Jonathan didn't mind too much because the mouse told him such interesting things about the attic. It wasn't a proper attic with stairs—you had to climb through a trap door in the ceiling to get to it, so of course Jonathan had never seen it.

"Is it dark up there?" asked Jonathan.

"Yes, very," said the mouse, "with dust and cobwebs everywhere."

"Dust and cobwebs?" asked Jonathan in amazement, thinking of his mother's busy vacuum cleaner, "in *our* house?"

"All over the place," answered the mouse, "and lots of spiders."

"I don't think I'd like our attic," said Jonathan.

"No," said the mouse, "the doll's house is much superior. That's why I come. *I* have more sense than to stay in a dusty attic when I could be living in a doll's house."

The mouse may have more sense, thought Jonathan to himself, but it certainly doesn't have many manners. One night when it was *very* rude, Jonathan decided to scare it a bit. "Elizabeth is asking for a pet," he said. "She wants a cat."

"A cat!" squawked the mouse, dropping the cookie it was eating. It looked around nervously. "Who is Elizabeth?"

"My big sister."

"Humph!" said the mouse. "Girls! People girls!"

At that Jonathan relented. "Don't worry," he said kindly. "Mother said she'd have to wait until after we have our holidays. You'll be outside being a field mouse before then."

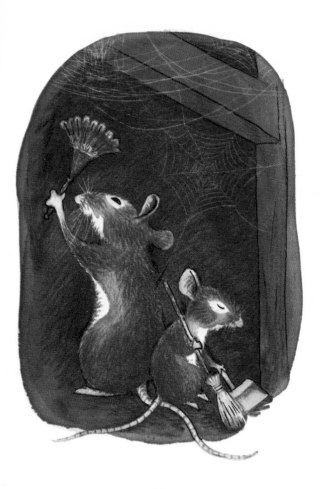

But the mouse was very upset and refused to talk to Jonathan any more that night.

Then one day Jonathan happened to look out the window. He noticed that the snow had almost disappeared from the garden and that the sun was drying the patio. It will soon be spring, he thought. Will the mouse go back to the fields now?

Jonathan wondered about this for a few moments. Then suddenly he remembered the little football Father had given him in the fall. It had lain in the toy box all winter. Jonathan found it and took it outside. He couldn't kick it very far. But he kept trying and after a while he could kick it a bit better.

He played outside with the little football all afternoon and had no nap—and so that night he just could not make himself get up to visit with the mouse. He sat up in bed, yawning sleepily, and looked over towards the doll's house. "Hello, Mouse," he said, "I'm awfully sleepy tonight."

"Are you?" said the mouse, standing at the front edge of the doll's house. "Well, don't worry about me. I can look after myself. Just as long as you left some cookies."

"I did," said Jonathan sleepily, and lay down on his pillow again.

The next day was Saturday. Jonathan went to his father. "Will you show me how to kick my football?" he asked. Father was pleased, and he and Jonathan played outside in the garden with it all afternoon. Jonathan was so hungry when he came in that he ate all his cookies himself—he was just too hungry to save any in his pocket for the mouse.

And that night Jonathan slept right through the night—he didn't wake up at all.

Gosh, thought Jonathan in the morning, the mouse will be angry with me.

And it was. The next night, when Jonathan did get up, it wouldn't speak to him at all. Jonathan had left its favorite kind of cookie—chocolate chip—and made himself get out of bed to kneel by the doll's house. But the mouse only squeaked rather angrily in Jonathan's direction and turned its back on him while it gobbled up the cookie.

Jonathan was puzzled. Was the mouse not going to talk to him any more? Or . . . was it perhaps . . . that Jonathan just couldn't *understand* the mouse any more?

Jonathan thought about this for several days. He woke up in the night a few times to see whether the mouse was willing to talk again, but he found it harder and harder to get out of his warm cosy bed. One night he wasn't even sure whether he saw the mouse in the doll's house at all—and he was too sleepy to get out of bed and check.

42

I wonder if it has gone back to being a field mouse, thought Jonathan, and asked his mother if it was spring yet.

"Yes, it's spring," answered Mother. "The robins are back and I saw a crocus in the garden yesterday."

It must have gone back to the fields, thought Jonathan. I know—I'll tidy the doll's house all up. Then I'll be able to tell if the mouse is still living in it.

Jonathan made up the little bed very neatly and swept out the whole house. He set the little red chairs around the table and put all the bits of velvet rug in their proper places. And he left one chocolate cookie by the little stairs.

The next morning nothing had been touched. The chairs were in their places, the bed was still tidy, and the cookie was still there. Jonathan looked at the little house for a long time. If the cookie is still there, that means the mouse *must* have gone, he thought. The mouse would never leave a whole cookie, no matter how angry it was. While he was thinking, Jonathan nibbled at the cookie hungrily. I may as well eat it myself then, he decided. And he did. He was always hungry these days.

That afternoon Jonathan said to Father, "If you want, you can put the doll's house back in Elizabeth's room now."

"Don't you want it any more?" asked Father.

"No, thank you," answered Jonathan. "I've finished with it."

44

But Elizabeth had a new desk in her room where the doll's house had stood—there wasn't any room for it now. So Father carried the doll's house down to the basement and put it away in the corner along with the old baby carriage and the outgrown skates.

Jonathan sat on the basement stairs and looked at the little house, sitting there deserted in the corner.

I wonder if the mouse will come looking for its house next winter, he thought. He worried about this for a moment. Then he smiled. Well if it does, I'll just tell it where the house is now, he decided. The mouse can just as easily live in it down here.

And without looking at the little house again, Jonathan ran outside to practice kicking his football some more.

Date Due